corgi of justice

by Elyse Beaudette

chapter 1
getting
adopted.

4

5

Chapter 2 The walk.

9

Chapter 3
The fight!

12

13

14

19

Chapter 4
Going home

DING Dong!

chapter 5

the aunt

fever!

25

26

Chapter 6
Corgi gone wrong!

31

34

35

Chapter 7

Give me marley!

38

44

45

Chapter 8
THE
KIDNAPPER!

47

48

49

51

54

56

Chapter 9
The baby!

58

Billy is playful!

Billy is happy

Billy is family.

Billy likes to scribble oh paper.

Billy loves us! ♡

61

Chapter 10
The end.
)))

The end

Elyse Beaudette is a girl who lives in New Hampshire and loves to draw. She enjoys drawing things like dogs, cats and people. The character "Murphy" in her book is based off of her real life cat with the same name! Elyse was diagnosed with cystic fibrosis at birth. She raises money for CF with her family by participating in a walk every year and it means a lot to her. A tip from Elyse is "if you ever want to do anything, make it positive!"

ISBN: 978-1-937721-95-4

Publisher by
Peter E. Randall Publisher
5 Greenleaf Woods Drive, Suite 102
Portsmouth, NH 03801
www.perpublisher.com

Printed in the United States of America